Roots of Wonder
Moral Stories for Children

Learning Values, Celebrating Festivals & Building Kind Hearts

Igniting Courage, Wisdom & Wonder

Dr. Vivek B. Naik

Clever Fox® PUBLISHING
Chennai • Bangalore

CLEVER FOX PUBLISHING
Chennai, India

Published by CLEVER FOX PUBLISHING 2026

ISBN: 978-93-344-4142-0

DEDICATION

For my beloved daughters, Rajvi & Parishi

the shining hearts who inspire every page of this series. You are the true heroes of these stories, and through you, I rediscover the wonder of roots, courage, and love.

For my wife Janki

whose love and guidance nurture our children, teaching them to live their values. Watching you with them inspired me to write these stories, so that other families too can learn and grow together.

For my family

Dr. Bhadresh Naik (DADU) and Jayashree Naik (DADI) who showed me that roots are not only remembered but practiced every single day.

For the teachers and schools

who plant these seeds of wisdom in every child, keeping our culture alive for generations to come.

Dr. Vivek B. Naik

INTRODUCTION: WHY ROOTS MATTER

Our roots are like the banyan tree
strong, deep, and full of life.
Hindu roots are not just old traditions;
they are living values that guide us every day.
Through stories, festivals, and daily acts,
Rajvi, Parishi, and their little friend Chintu
discover that courage, kindness, patience, and
respect make life more joyful and meaningful.

This book invites children (and families) to:

Learn from Hindu stories and values.

Feel — the emotions behind patience, courage, and kindness.

Do — fun activities that bring roots alive at home or school.

Let's begin this journey — from big festivals to small daily acts—and discover how our Hindu roots keep us strong, loving, and bright.

Dr. Vivek B. Naik

WHAT THIS BOOK IS ALL ABOUT

"Roots of Wonder" helps children rediscover Hindu roots as living values, not just traditions. Through the daily lives of Rajvi, Parishi, and their little friend Chintu, the book connects festivals, prayers, and small daily actions with universal values like kindness, courage, gratitude, patience, honesty, and respect.

Each short story blends:

cultural elements (like Karagre Vasate Lakshmi, Hanuman's leap, or Krishna's prank), a modern child's situation (like school, play, or home moments), and concludes with a reflection question and a simple creative activity that turns learning into action. It is not just a storybook — it's a values workbook and a family conversation guide.

HOW PARENTS AND TEACHERS CAN USE THIS BOOK

This book is designed for interactive reading, not passive storytelling. Here's how parents and educators can make the most of it:

1. Read Together

Each story takes just a few minutes. Read it aloud, pause after key moments, and ask your child:
"What do you think Rajvi felt here?"
"What would you do if this happened to you?"

2. Discuss Reflection Questions

Every page ends with a question that encourages emotional thinking and self-awareness. Parents can use these to talk about real-life situations — like honesty, forgiveness, or patience — in a safe, loving way.

3. Do the Activities

The creative activities (like drawing a "Blessing Hand," making a "Values Star," or building a "Family Tree") reinforce the message through art and play. Teachers can use these as classroom projects, and families can do them on weekends or festival days.

4. Relate to Festivals

During Diwali, Holi, Raksha Bandhan, or Ganesh Chaturthi revisit the related pages. Let children connect rituals with meanings, not just celebrations.

HOW IT HELPS KIDS

Builds emotional intelligence — through reflection and empathy. Strengthens moral reasoning — by linking choices with values. Encourages creativity and curiosity — through art-based activities. Fosters cultural confidence — helping children understand their roots with pride, not pressure. Supports spiritual balance through simple daily practices, such as gratitude, patience, and forgiveness. Children learn that Hinduism is not about doing, but about being — kind, respectful, courageous, and calm.

HOW IT STRENGTHENS FAMILY BONDING

Each story becomes a conversation bridge between generations: Grandparents can share their own experiences ("When I was small, my mother said this prayer..."). Parents can guide with gentle meaning ("We light diyas to spread kindness"). Children can ask freely and express their feelings. When families sit together to read, draw, chant, or discuss — they create shared memories rooted in love and learning. It transforms rituals into relationships and festivals into family reflections.

Page Element	How Parents/Elders Can Expand
Anchor Line	Explain the deeper value simply — e.g.,"Hanuman's courage came from his love for Ram, not just muscles.
Emotional Highlight	Talk about similar feelings the child had that week — "When were you scared but still brave?"
Little Life Lesson	Share a real-life example — "Remember when you helped Dadi with pooja? That was seva.
Reflection Question	Encourage open talk — let the child think, don't correct.
Activity	Sit together and complete it — help draw, color, or act it out. Praise the child's effort, not the neatness.

AS AN AUTHOR, HOW YOU CAN EXPLAIN THE PURPOSE YOU CAN SAY:

"My goal in writing this book was not to teach religion, but to awaken values.
I want parents, teachers, and elders to use these stories as a path — not to give answers, but to start conversations.
Every reflection question, every activity, every page is a door to a deeper talk between you and your child.
You don't need to cover everything — just one story a day can plant a seed of gratitude, courage, or kindness.
My role as an author ends with giving you that seed — the real magic happens when you nurture it with your child."

IN SHORT — THIS BOOK IS:

For	Helps With	Method
Children (4–10 yrs)	Values, emotions, cultural awareness	Stories + Art + Reflection
Parents & Teachers	Bonding, communication, teaching empathy	Guided discussion & activities
Families	Passing culture with love	Reading together

Morning Roots: Karagre Vasate Lakshmi

Rajvi woke up early, stretched, and gently nudged her sister.

Anchor : Morning prayers remind us that strength, wisdom, and blessings begin with us.

Emotional Highlight : Sleepy → Peaceful & Ready for the Day

Little Life Lesson : When we start the day with gratitude, everything feels brighter.

It means : "Maa Lakshmi resides in the top part of the hand, Mata Saraswati resides in the middle part, and Shri Govinda resides in the bottom part of the hand. Therefore, the first thing you should do after waking up in the morning is to look at your palms."

Reflection Question : "What's one small thing you're thankful for when you wake up?"

Activity : Trace your palm on paper. Inside the fingers, draw symbols of Lakshmi (lotus), Saraswati (veena/book), and Govinda (flute). Color them to make your "Blessing Hand."

Daily Roots: Morning Pooja with Mumma

Rajvi and Parishi stand neatly in their school uniforms in front of the glowing home mandir.

Anchor : Morning pooja roots the day in respect, gratitude, and strength.

Emotional Highlight : Eager → Peaceful & Blessed.

Little Life Lesson : "Starting the day with prayer gives courage, calmness, and joy."

Reflection Question : "What do you want to pray for before your day begins?"

Activity : Draw your own morning ritual — maybe lighting a diya, folding hands, or standing with your family in front of your mandir.

Roots in Respect: Namaste & Blessings

Rajvi and Parishi stand ready with their school bags. They join their palms and bow slightly, "Namaste, Dadu! Namaste, Dadi !"

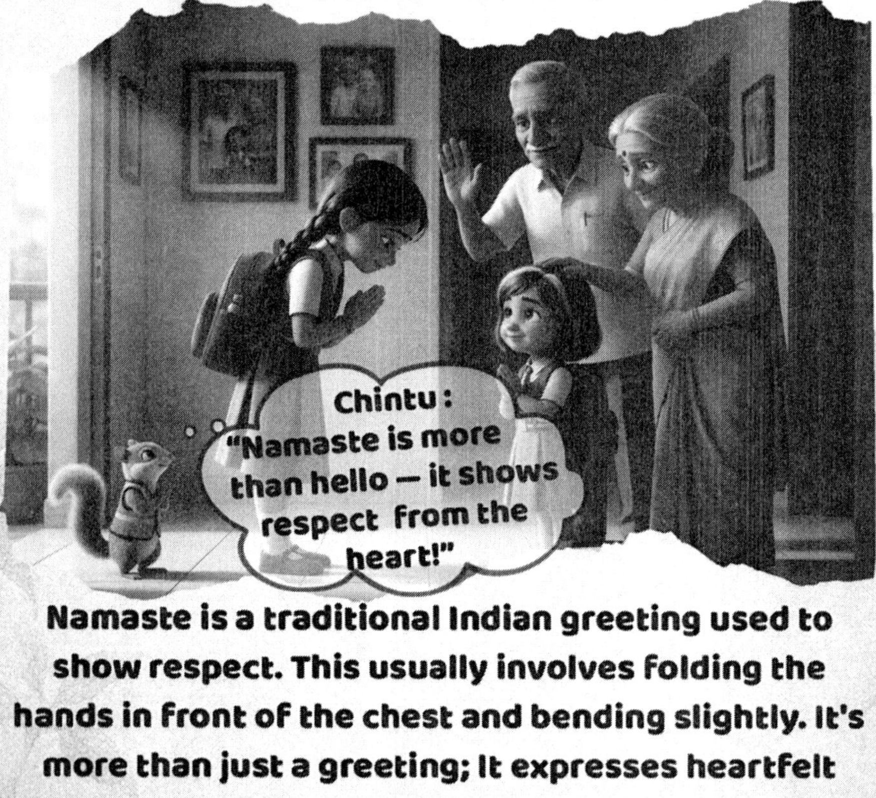

Namaste is a traditional Indian greeting used to show respect. This usually involves folding the hands in front of the chest and bending slightly. It's more than just a greeting; It expresses heartfelt respect.

Anchor : Respect for elders through greetings and blessings strengthens family bonds.

Emotional Highlight : Loved → Guided & Protected.

Little Life Lesson : "Namaste is a way of honoring the divine in others."

Reflection Question : "Who do you greet with respect every day — and how does it make them feel?"

Activity : Practice saying Namaste with your palms joined. Then write or draw the blessings you receive from elders.

Roots in Learning: Saraswati's Blessing

Learning is sacred — Saraswati teaches us to honor knowledge with respect and joy. It's exam morning. Rajvi places her notebook gently before Saraswati Maa's photo. Parishi whispers, "Books are like blessings, aren't they?" Chintu: "Shhh... even pencils sing when Saraswati smiles!"

Anchor : Learning is sacred — Saraswati teaches us to honor knowledge with respect and joy.

Emotional Highlight : Nervous → Confident.

Little Life Lesson : "Respecting books and learning invites wisdom."

Reflection Question: "What's one subject or skill that feels like Saraswati's blessing to you?"

Activity: Decorate the cover of your favorite notebook with symbols of Saraswati — a veena, lotus, or swan.

Roots in Values: Living Them at School

At school, Rajvi notices a classmate without lunch. She quickly offers half of hers. Parishi helps another friend pack away books that fell down. Chintu (clapping tiny paws): "Values are like sunshine — they glow wherever you carry them!"

Anchor: Hindu roots remind us that values like kindness and honesty must be practised daily, everywhere.

Emotional Highlight : Helpful → Appreciated.

Little Life Lesson: "Real values show in small actions at school, home, and play."

Reflection Question : "What's one kind or honest thing you did in school recently?"

Activity : Make a "Value Star." On each point, write one value you try to practice (like kindness, honesty, sharing, respect, patience).

Rama's Dharma: Doing the Right Thing

Rajvi notices a shiny pencil under her desk.

Anchor : Rama shows us that honesty is the strongest path.

Emotional Highlight : Tempted → Proud.

Little Life Lesson: "Doing the right thing may be tough, but it always feels good inside."

Rajvi walks up and returns the pencil to the teacher, feeling proud.

Reflection Question : "When did you return something that wasn't yours?"

Activity : Make a "Dharma Tree." On each branch, write one honest or fair choice you can make this week.

Krishna's Raas: Dance of Friendship

At recess, Rajvi sits alone, watching as Jiaansh runs to cricket and Hayaan joins football.

She whispers sadly: "No one wants to play with me..."

Anchor: Krishna reminds us that friendship is about joy, togetherness, and including everyone.

Emotional Highlight: Lonely → Joyfully connected.

Little Life Lesson: "Real friendship makes space for everyone."

Parishi takes her hand with a smile: "In Krishna's raas, everyone is part of the circle!"
She calls: "Come here, let's play together!"
Soon, all friends join hands, spinning, laughing, and dancing in a big circle.

Reflection Question: "Have you ever seen someone alone? How could you include them in your game?"

Activity: Draw a "Friendship Circle." Inside the circle, write your friends' names — and add one more space for someone new to join.

Saraswati's Song: Wisdom in Creativity

Rajvi frowns at her school project: "It's too hard! Nothing looks right..."

Chintu (playing a small veena, with shining eyes): "When hard work and thinking dance together, wisdom sings!"

Anchor : Saraswati teaches us to learn with joy, not fear.

Emotional Highlight : Frustrated → Inspired.

Little Life Lesson : "Wisdom flows when you relax and create with joy."

Rajvi takes a deep breath, starts sketching
while humming along. Soon
her ideas sparkle onto the page.

Mumma sits beside
her, humming softly:
"Saraswati flows like a river,
beti. Knowledge comes when
we let it flow — not when we
block it."

Reflection Question: "What helps you when you're
stuck on something hard?"
Activity : Make your own "Wisdom Song" —
write a rhyme, doodle, or small poem
that makes learning fun.

Krishna's Butter Prank: Forgiveness Turns Sweet

Parishi sneaks Rajvi's chocolate without asking.

Anchor : Krishna teaches us to balance fun with kindness.

Emotional Highlight : Angry → Loving.

Little Life Lesson : "Mistakes happen — Forgiveness makes hearts close again."

Reflection Question: "Have you ever forgiven someone after they made you upset?"

Activity: Draw a butter pot. Inside, write or draw ways to say sorry to a friend or sibling.

Hanuman's Leap: Courage and Devotion

At the park, Parishi stares at the tall slide, nervous.

Anchor: Hanuman shows us courage comes from devotion and faith.

Emotional Highlight: Scared → Brave.

Little Life Lesson : "Courage is not the absence of fear — it's moving forward with love."

Parishi takes a deep breath, pushes off — and zooms down laughing!

Reflection Question : "What's one brave thing you tried recently, even though you were scared?"

Activity: Make a paper 'Courage Medal' wear it whenever you do something brave.

Sita's Strength: Patience and Purity

At the park, Parishi pouts at the swing.

Anchor: Sita teaches us that patience and self-respect make us strong inside.

Emotional Highlight: Restless → Calm.

Little Life Lesson: "Patience is powerful — it gives you quiet strength."

Parishi takes a deep breath, she realises after waiting calmly,

Reflection Question: "When was a time you waited calmly and felt proud afterward?"

Activity: Draw your own 'Patience Circle' — each time you wait calmly (for your turn, food, or play), color in one part.

Shiva's Dance: Starting Fresh

Rajvi and Parishi are building a tall block tower. Suddenly—CRASH!—the tower falls to the ground.

Anchor: Shiva reminds us that starting fresh can bring balance and joy.

Emotional Highlight: Upset → Excited.

Little Life Lesson: "When something breaks, it's not the end — it's the beginning of something new."

The girls laugh, pick up the blocks, and build a new tower — taller and steadier than before.

Reflection Question: "Have you ever made something again, and it turned out even better?"

Activity: Play the "tower game" — build with blocks, knock it down, and rebuild in a new way.

Ganesha's Big Ears: Listening with Love

At dinner, Rajvi is telling a funny story. Parishi interrupts three times with her own comments.

Anchor: Ganesha teaches us that real listening makes others feel loved and valued.

Emotional Highlight: Frustrated → Heard.

Little Life Lesson: "Listening with love is a superpower."

Parishi nods and waits quietly as Rajvi finishes her story.

Reflection Question: "When did you feel happy because someone really listened to you?"

Activity: Play the "listening game" — one person tells a short story for 2 minutes while the other only listens without interrupting. Then switch!

Roots in the Sun: Light of Gratitude

Anchor: The Sun reminds us to begin each day with gratitude.

Emotional Highlight: Sleepy → Energized

Little Life Lesson: "Gratitude brings light into our day."

Rajvi and Parishi step outside. The golden rays touch their faces.

The girls raise their hands too, smiling.

Reflection Question: "What's one gift the Sun gives us that you love?"

Activity: Draw the Sun and write one thank you on each ray (light, warmth, food, playtime...).

Roots in Sound: Power of Om

Parishi bangs on a steel plate, making a racket.

Anchor: Mantras like Om remind us that sound can heal and guide us.

Emotional Highlight: Noisy → Calm

Little Life Lesson: "Peaceful sounds bring peaceful feelings."

She closes her eyes and chants softly: "Om..."
The room suddenly feels calm.
Rajvi and Parishi try it too, giggling first, then smiling as the sound hums in their chest.

Reflection Question: "What sound from nature makes you feel peaceful?"

Activity: Try "bee breathing" — close your eyes, hum like a bee, and notice how your head feels calm.

Roots in Food: Respect Every Bite

At dinner, Parishi leaves half her chapati on the plate.

Anchor: Food is sacred — wasting it wastes blessings.

Emotional Highlight: Careless → Grateful

Little Life Lesson: "Take only what you need, finish with respect."

Together they fold hands, whisper a short thank-you, and finish happily.

Reflection Question: "Who all helped bring food to your plate?"

Activity: Make a "Food Gratitude Chain" — draw Sun → rain → farmer → cook → your plate.

Roots in Nature: Earth's Superheroes

Rajvi kicks an empty chips packet on the ground.

Anchor: Protecting nature makes us Earth's superheroes.

Emotional Highlight: Careless → Responsible

Little Life Lesson: "Every small choice keeps nature safe."

They pick it up, put it in the bin, and water the park tree instead.

Reflection Question: "If you were Earth's superhero, what power would you use to protect it?"

Activity: "Nature Hero Badge" — draw a leaf or tree, color it, and wear it proudly.

Roots in Helping: Seva is Worship

The family is serving food at a community lunch. Rajvi hurries and spills dal on the floor. Parishi bends down to clean. "Helping is not only serving, it's also caring."

Anchor: Helping others is seva — it turns kindness into prayer.

Emotional Highlight: Careless → Caring

Little Life Lesson: "Every act of help, small or big, is sacred."

Reflection Question: "Who did you help today, and how did it feel?"

Activity: Make a "Helping Hands List" with your family. Write one way each person will help this week (serving food, carrying bags, feeding someone, cleaning).

Roots in Truth & Ahimsa – Courage with Kindness

At the park, a group of kids blames the watchman uncle: "He broke the swing!" Rajvi knows the truth — she saw a boy leaning too hard.

Anchor : Satya and Ahimsa mean speaking the truth with love, not anger.

Emotional Highlight: Fearful → Courageous & Kind

Little Life Lesson: "Real strength is being honest without hurting others."

The group nods, the boy feels safe, and the watchman uncle smiles gratefully.

Reflection Question : "Can you think of a time you told the truth gently?"

Activity : With a friend or sibling, practice saying one hard truth in a soft way (e.g., "I didn't like when you grabbed my toy — can we share instead?").

Roots in Hospitality : Welcoming with Love

On a hot afternoon, a delivery man rings the bell. Rajvi quickly grabs the parcel and shuts the door.

Anchor: Atithi Devo Bhava means treating every guest with warmth.

Emotional Highlight: Rushed → Welcoming

Little Life Lesson: "A smile, a glass of water, or a kind word can be worship."

Parishi runs to bring a glass. The man drinks gratefully and says, "Your home feels so kind."

Reflection Question: "How do you welcome someone who comes to your door?"

Activity: Make a "Welcome Card" or draw a diya to keep near your door for guests.

Roots in Forgiveness: Kshama is Cool

At the park, a boy splashes mud on Parishi's dress by mistake.

Anchor: Forgiveness cools anger and keeps peace.

Emotional Highlight: Forgiveness — feeling happy

Little Life Lesson: "Strong hearts forgive faster."

Reflection Question: "How does forgiving make you feel?"

Activity: Make a "Cool Heart" — draw a blue heart and write one name you choose to forgive inside.

Roots in Holi: Colors of Forgiveness

Rajvi and Parishi stand with water balloons, glaring at each other from their fight. Papa suddenly splashes both with blue! "No — it's forgiveness!"

Anchor: Holi is the festival of washing away anger with colors of love.

Emotional Highlight: Angry → Joyful

Little Life Lesson: "Forgiving makes life colorful again."

Reflection Question: "What color do you think forgiveness feels like?"

Activity: Draw a family rainbow — each person chooses one color that shows love.

Roots in Raksha Bandhan: Bonds that Protect

Anchor: Raksha Bandhan teaches us to protect each other with love.

Emotional Highlight: Playful → Proud

Little Life Lesson: "Protection is not one-sided — it flows both ways."

Just then, cousins Hayaan and Jiaansh rush in: "What about us?" Rajvi and Parishi giggle, tying rakhis on them too. Papa passes the sweets, and soon everyone is teasing, laughing, and celebrating together.

Reflection Question: "Who makes you feel safe, and how do you protect them back?"

Activity: Make a paper rakhi and tie it to someone you care about — brother, sister, cousin, or friend.

Roots in Ganesh Chaturthi: Loving Bappa, Loving Nature

Parishi looks at their clay Ganesha idol and frowns.

Anchor: Ganesh Chaturthi reminds us that real devotion means protecting both Bappa and the world he loves.

Emotional Highlight: Sad → Happy

Little Life Lesson: "When we care for nature, we carry Bappa's blessing in every step."

Reflection Question: "What's one way you can protect nature, just like keeping Bappa's rivers and trees safe?"

Activity: Make a tiny eco-friendly Ganesha out of clay/playdough and share one promise you'll keep for nature (like saving water, planting a tree, or avoiding plastic).

Roots in Navratri: Strength in Devotion

The cousins dress up for garba.

Anchor: Navratri is not just about dancing — it's about courage and devotion.

Emotional Highlight: anxiety → confidence, shyness → excitement

Little Life Lesson: "When we face life with courage and faith, every fear becomes a dance step."

Rajvi smiles, finally joins, and soon the circle glows with laughter and rhythm.

Reflection Question: "What's one fear you can dance past if Maa Durga gave you courage?"

Activity: "Courage Sticks" — decorate two pencils or sticks, write a brave word (like faith, honesty, love), and clap them when you need courage.

Roots in Lakshmi's Light: Sharing with Joy

Anchor: Diwali reminds us that kindness and generosity create joy.

Emotional Highlight: Greedy → Joyful

Little Life Lesson: "Happiness multiplies when we share."

The kids pause, then break the sweets and share bites with each other. Soon the room fills with giggles.

Reflection Question: "What's something small you shared that made both of you smile?"

Activity: Make a "Sharing Circle" — draw a diya flame and write inside 3 things you will share this week (toys, time, sweets, smiles).

Roots in Diwali: Victory of Light

The cousins run outside with diyas.

Anchor: Diwali reminds us that light and goodness always win over darkness.

Emotional Highlight: Fear of dark → Joy of light

Little Life Lesson: "Even one small light can chase away a lot of darkness."

Reflection Question: "What's your little light — kindness, smile, or bravery?"

Activity: Draw a diya and inside its flame write one good quality you promise to shine with.

Roots in Family: Our Own Trees

Rajvi and Parishi sit under the big neem tree near their house.

Anchor: Family is our tree — roots give us strength, branches help us grow.

Emotional Highlight: Curious → Engaged.

Little Life Lesson: "Families keep us grounded, yet help us reach higher."

Reflection Question: "Who in your family feels like roots, and who feels like branches?"

Activity: Put roots, trunk, branches, and leaves, and write each family member's name in a part.

Modern Roots: Unity in Diversity

At the school fair, Rajvi sees children in different clothes — one with a tilak, one with a cap, one with a cross.

Anchor: Our roots teach us to respect all paths and live as one family.

Emotional Highlight: Curious → Accepting.

Little Life Lesson: "Diversity is beautiful when held together by respect."

Reflection Question: "How can you show love to someone who prays differently from you?"

Activity: Create a "Unity Poster" featuring symbols from various religions.

Roots Around the World: How Others Teach the Same Values

Every faith teaches love, honesty, kindness, and courage — just like the stories we have learned in Roots of Wonder.

Though the names and traditions are different, the light of goodness shines the same everywhere.

Christianity: Jesus taught forgiveness — just like Krishna forgave his friends.

Islam: Prophet Muhammad taught honesty and kindness — just like Rama's truth and fairness.

Sikhism: Guru Nanak taught seva (service) — the same spirit as helping others in our stories.

Buddhism: Buddha showed calm and compassion — like Sita's patience.

Jainism: Mahavira taught Ahimsa — kindness to all beings.

Reflection Question: What's one lesson that connects all these roots?

Global Roots Activity Page —
"All Values, One World Tree"
Draw a big tree on your page.
In the roots, write the values you have learned:
Kindness, Truth, Respect,
Gratitude, Courage, Forgiveness.
In the branches, draw or color symbols from different faiths — (Hinduism), (Christianity), (Islam), (Sikhism), (Buddhism), (Judaism).
In the leaves, write small actions that show these values
in real life — like sharing, helping, or forgiving.
Different roots, same light — we all grow from goodness.

GLOBAL VALUES ACTIVITY — "ALL VALUES, ONE WORLD TREE"

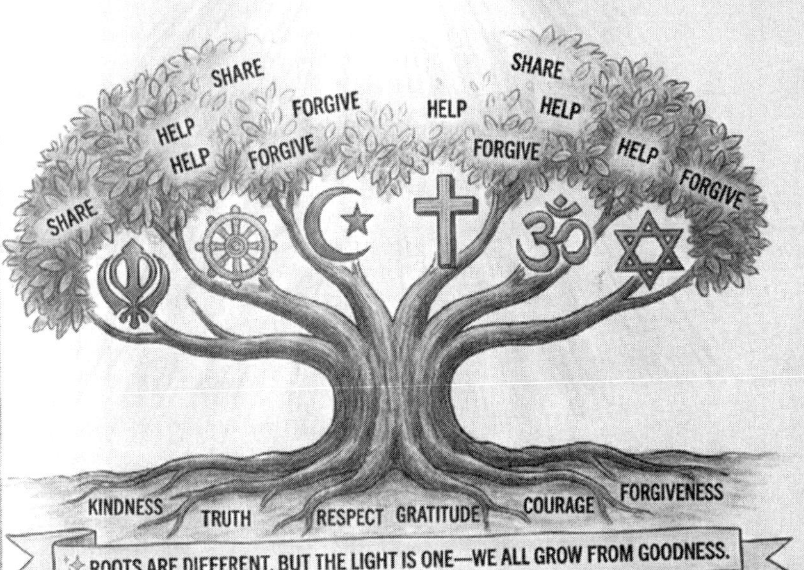

Wrap-Up: Heroes of Our Roots

Back under the glowing banyan tree.

Parishi: "We've seen so many roots!"

Rajvi: "And they're all inside us.

"Dadu: "Yes — roots are not just in the past.

They live when you practice them."

"You're now our Roots Heroes!"

Anchor: "Our Hindu roots are living values that guide us every day."

Reflection Question: "Which root will you live today?

Activity: Receive your "Roots Hero" certificate (closing page).

Roots Hero Award

CERTIFICATE OF HONOR

This is to proudly certify that
is a true Roots Hero!

For living the values of our Hindu roots — kindness, respect, courage, and devotion — and for carrying them into today's world.

Signed with blessings,
Dadu, Dadi, Mama, Papa, and Chintu

Glossary: Words from Roots of Wonder

Dharma	: Doing what's right, like being honest or fair.
Diya	: A morning prayer for blessings of wealth, wisdom, and strength.
Karagre Vasate Lakshmi	: Forgiving others to stay calm and kind.
Kshama	: A special place at home or a temple for prayer.
Mandir	: A greeting with folded hands to show respect.
Namaste	: A sacred sound that brings peace when chanted.
Om	: Praying with flowers or lamps to thank God.
Prasad	: Food offered to God, shared as a blessing.
Rakhi	: A thread tied during Raksha Bandhan to show love and protection.
Seva	: Helping others with love, like serving food.
Ahimsa	: Being kind and not hurting others with words or actions.
Values	: Good qualities learned from home and elders. Like Rajvi speaks kindly to everyone.
Compassion	: Understanding others' pain and helping them.

A QUIET CLOSING THOUGHT

If this book helped even one child pause,
feel, or ask a question —
then its purpose is fulfilled.
Roots don't grow overnight.
They grow through small moments —
a story read before bed,
a question asked without fear,
a value practiced without being taught.
You don't need to remember every page.
You don't need to explain everything perfectly.
If this book opened even one honest conversation in your home,
it has already done its work.
Thank you for reading slowly,
and with heart.

— Dr. Vivek B. Naik

THE JOURNEY CONTINUES

Roots of Wonder is the beginning of a larger journey with Rajvi, Parishi, and their little friend Chintu.
As children grow, new questions appear — about feelings, mistakes, safety, differences, and the world around them.
This series follows those questions, gently and honestly.

Books in the Series

1. **Roots of Wonder**
   Exploring values, culture, kindness, and everyday wisdom through stories and festivals.
2. **When Worry Visits**
   Helping children understand worries and learn calm, courage, and emotional safety.
3. **When Adults Make Mistakes**
   Showing how apologies, accountability, and repair build trust and love.
4. **My Body, My Rules**
   Teaching body awareness, consent, and safety with clarity and care.
5. **Big Feelings, Brave Hearts**
   Helping children name, express, and manage strong emotions.
6. **Private Means Private**
   Understanding personal boundaries, secrets, and safe sharing.
7. **Brain Types Are Beautiful**
   Celebrating different ways of thinking, learning, and being.
8. **When the World Feels Too Much**
   Tools for overwhelm, sensitivity, and emotional regulation.
9. **Digital Danger, Strong Mind**
   Guiding children through screens, online spaces, and digital safety.

You may read them in order —
or begin wherever your child's questions are today.

🎨 **A GIFT FOR YOUR CHILD**

FREE ROOTS OF WONDER ACTIVITY BOOK

If your child enjoyed these stories, we've created a free printable activity companion to continue the journey.

The Roots of Wonder Activity Book includes:

• coloring pages

• drawing and reflection prompts

• simple games and puzzles

• family and culture-based activities

It's designed to be optional, playful, and child-led —

not homework.

📩 To receive the free activity book, please write to us at:

rajviparishiadventure@gmail.com

We'll email you the printable pages so you can enjoy them

at your own pace, whenever it feels right.

🤍 THANK YOU FOR BEING PART OF THIS JOURNEY

This book was written from
real family moments —
questions asked, mistakes made,
values lived.
If you choose to continue this
journey with us,
you are always welcome.
Read slowly.
Talk openly.
Grow together.